Books by Sarah Price

The Amish of Lancaster Series
#1 Fields of Corn
#2 Hills of Wheat
#3 Pastures of Faith
#4 Valley of Hope

The Amish of Ephrata Series
#1 The Tomato Patch
#2 The Quilting Bee

The Adventures of a Family Dog Series
#1 A Small Dog Named Peek-a-boo
#2 Peek-a-boo Runs Away
#3 Peek-a-boo's New Friends
#4 Peek-a-boo and Daisy Doodle

Other Books
Gypsy in Black

Find Sarah Price on Facebook and Goodreads!
Learn about upcoming books, sequels, series, and contests!

The Tomato Patch:
The Amish of Ephrata

An Amish Novella on Morality

By
Sarah Price

Published by Price Publishing, LLC.
Morristown, New Jersey
2012

The Pennsylvania Dutch used in this manuscript is taken from the Pennsylvania Dutch Revised Dictionary (1991) by C. Richard Beam, Brookshire Publications, Inc. in Lancaster, PA.

Contact the author on Facebook at
http://www.facebook.com/fansofsarahprice or
visit her Web Blog at http://sarahpriceauthor.wordpress.com.

Price Publishing, LLC.
Morristown, NJ
http://www.pricepublishing.org

Dedicated to anyone who has ever experienced bullying, whether in person or on the Internet. It is my wish that people will read this book and recognize that false accusations, lies, and general bad will against others are clearly not Christian behavior.

This novella is dedicated to Pam and Sue, administrators of the Whoopie Pie Book Club Group on Facebook, whose sense of diplomacy and moral values are exemplary.

Chapter One

Priscilla Smucker stood on the edge of the garden, staring at the neat rows of pretty tomato plants that poked up from the ground. Their green leaves stretched toward the warm spring sun. There was no place she'd rather be than standing barefoot in the middle of her tomato patch. The feel of the dirt on her feet and the smell of freshly growing vegetables surrounding her always made her happy. She shut her eyes and breathed in deeply, enjoying the moment as she envisioned the garden in full glory, come late June and early July.

But it was only the first week of June. It would be at least four weeks before the growing plants produced any edible vegetables. In the meantime, Priscilla would continue to work in the tomato patch, tending to each plant as if it were a child and she, the nurturing mother.

Springtime on her daed's farm was always her favorite time of year. Crops were planted and grew. Cows gave birth to their calves. Life was born anew on the farm. But, for Priscilla, she loved gardening more than anything, including canning, haying, and caring for the newborn calves. It made her feel good to work with the earth, creating something from nothing, something that would be enjoyed by her family while experiencing a spiritual connection with God.

During this first week of June, the air was more like spring than summer. Priscilla's brown hair was covered with a blue bandana. She wiped at her forehead, feeling the beads of perspiration, not from heat but from hard work. Yet, she didn't mind. For the past six weeks, she had been tending to the garden, first plowing the patch of ground, then mixing in composted manure to make the soil rich and ready for the plants. Finally, she had planned the layout of the garden and planted her seeds. Tending to the garden was something she had looked forward to throughout the cold winter months.

A bird flew overhead, squawking as it dipped toward the stream behind her parents' house. It was almost time for dinner. Most days, the family gathered at twelve-thirty to share in the midday meal. She could tell time without looking at the sun overhead that it was almost that time. When her daed whistled from the dairy barn, she knew that he was almost done with his morning chores and would soon be headed into the house for the dinner meal.

Picking up her hoe in one hand and the bucket of weeds that she had just collected in another, Priscilla headed toward the house. She'd dump the weeds later in the compost pile that the family used behind the mule barn. For now, she wanted to clean up and help her mamm with setting up the table before her daed came in from the dairy barn.

"How's the garden?" her mamm asked as Priscilla walked into the kitchen and hurried to wash her hands at the sink. Her mamm handed her a fresh towel to dry them.

"*Gut*," Priscilla said. "Everything is growing nicely and I didn't see any sign of grubs this year." She glanced over her shoulder at the mess on the kitchen floor. An alphabet puzzle was scattered on the floor. A teddy bear was tossed casually on the torn green sofa against the wall. "You are watching Elsie's *kinner* again?"

Her mamm looked at the floor. She smiled and shook her head. "That little Katie is something else. She is a tornado, leaving a path of destruction behind her, ain't so?"

8

Without being asked, Priscilla hurried over to start picking up the toys and return them to the basket that her mamm kept for when her younger grandchildren came to visit. Elsie was her older sister and she lived across the street. On Thursdays and Fridays, she went to market in town and, on some of those days, their mamm watched her three young *kinner*.

It was nice to have the children around the house. As the youngest child and last daughter living at the home, Priscilla often felt lonely without her older siblings. But she knew that her mamm appreciated her help. Without Priscilla, her mamm would be the only one cooking for her daed and two older brothers who hadn't married yet.

Priscilla wiped down the table and set it for eight, putting the children on the one side next to where she always sat on the bench. Her mamm and daed would sit at the head of the old wooden kitchen table while her brothers were always seated opposite Priscilla. It was the routine in the house and, on an Amish farm, routine was everything. From rising every morning at four-thirty to milking the cows to worshipping God at a neighbor's house every other Sunday, there was very little that couldn't be predicted on the farm. Seasons came and went. Every year at the same time, fields were plowed, gardens were planted, hay was cut, corn was harvested, vegetables and fruits were preserved, cows were milked and meat was canned.

It always amazed Priscilla that some Amish youth wanted to explore the outside world, which was so full of unpredictability. She much preferred the quiet peace of the farm. Every day, something special happened that made her feel closer to God. From watching the birthing of calves to seeing the little birds at the birdfeeders that her mamm refilled every morning, life on a farm was the only life for Priscilla.

The door to the utility room opened and she heard her daed walk in, stomping his feet to kick off any loose dirt. Her older brothers would be following soon, she thought, and hurried over to pour fresh water into everyone's cup. On rare occasions, her mamm might make meadow tea, especially during the hot summer months. Usually it was just water for the adults and milk for the children.

"Go call the *kinner*, Priscilla," her mamm instructed gently. "They're playing on the back porch."

Slipping out the door at the back of the kitchen, Priscilla hurried through a small hallway to the porch. It was cooler there, during the warm days, as it was shaded by a large oak tree. The children loved to play there since they were free to make as much of a mess as they wanted. Hardly anyone else ever went back there.

"Katie, you get your brother and sister, now," Priscilla said softly. "Time to eat."

"Ach, we were all having so much fun," Katie whined but did as she was told.

"I can see that," Priscilla replied, quickly assessing the room. "Mayhaps we can pick this up together later tonight, surprise your *grossmammi,* ja?" She noticed that Katie glanced at her, her expression showing her lack of desire to surprise anyone. Priscilla raised an eyebrow, "I bet she'd sure tell your own mamm how helpful you were and that would make your mamm feel right gut, don't you think?"

Katie kicked at a small toy. "I reckon," she said then grabbed the hand of her little brother and started to walk toward the kitchen.

Priscilla smiled and motioned to her other niece that they should follow. Together, they entered the kitchen and took their places at the table. Priscilla sat next to the youngest one, Ben, in order to help him with his meal.

"Shall we pray?" her mamm said and all eight heads bowed down together for their moment of silent prayer.

As soon as their daed lifted his head, that was the signal that the meal could begin. The table was laden with fresh pickles, cabbage, applesauce, red beets, meatballs, boiled potatoes and chow-chow. There was cup cheese in one dish and apple butter in another, both of which would be lavishly spread across the fresh baked bread that their mamm had pulled out of the oven only an hour earlier. Dishes were passed, forks and knifes scrapped the plates, and the conversation began.

"Heard there's a charity dinner coming up in July," their daed said.

Priscilla looked up. Charity dinners were usually run by the Mennonite church. But the Amish liked to participate. "When is it, Daed?"

"Oh, let's see now," he said, tugging at his white beard and looking up at the ceiling. "Seem to recall hearing that it was mid-July. Going to be a vegetable contest, too." His eyes sparkled as he looked at Priscilla. "Jacob Byler told me about it. Seems his daughter, Susie, is going to enter her tomatoes in the contest."

"Now, why doesn't that surprise me?"

Priscilla glanced at her brother, Jonas. His tone hadn't been too friendly. Several years ago, her family had moved down to Florida from a different district in Pennsylvania. Her daed's parents were down there and were sickly. So Jacob Byler had uprooted his family to head south to care for them. Just last year, they had moved back north. His parents had passed and there wasn't much of a living to be made down in Sarasota, Florida.

It had only been about eighteen months since the Byler family had moved into the Smucker's church district. Priscilla was surprised that her brother would speak up about Susie Byler. "Why's that, brother?"

Eighteen-year old Jonas waved his hand in the air dismissively. "That Susie is always touting that her garden is the best and that she's the most famous Amish girl in the district for her tomatoes."

"That's idle gossip," their mamm said softly, a gentle reprimand to her son that he shouldn't speak about others in such a negative light.

"It's true," Jonas replied.

Their older brother, David nodded. "She's known to be a bit proud, Mamm."

Jonas continued. "And I bet Priscilla grows just as nice, if not better, tomatoes than that girl."

Mamm put down her fork and knife, staring at the boys. "What has gotten into you boys?" She looked at her husband. "Where are my sons? The ones that were raised properly and should know better than to speak unkindly about anyone?"

Priscilla tried to hide her smile as she saw her daed's mouth twitch, clearly fighting to keep a straight face. "Well, she sure does seem very prideful when it comes to those tomatoes," her daed said. "Her own father was repeating what she said and that seemed to be an awful lot of boasting."

David looked up. "Boasting? She was actually bragging that her tomatoes sold the most of any Amish farm in our district last year!"

"Seems she's more interested in making money than in growing good tomatoes and helping others," Daed added. When he saw his wife glare at him, he cleared his throat. "But your mamm's right. We should pray for her to see the error of her proud ways, no?"

Jonas tucked his head down and dove back into his food. "Oh I'll pray for her alright. Pray for her to move right back down to that Florida where her family came from!"

Mamm gasped. "Jonas!"

But the rest of the table laughed and even Mamm had to smile. It was no secret that since Susie Byler's family had moved to Ephrata, she had been making waves in the district. In the beginning, everyone had tried to deal with her fake smiles and overly dramatic concern over every person that she met. They chalked it up to Susie trying to make friends and find her way within the community. Moving from Florida to Pennsylvania was certainly a big change for a fourteen-year old. But, over the past two years, her dramatic ways had only seemed to increase. Priscilla was secretly thankful that she never had to attend school with her so her socialization was limited to Church Sundays and gatherings with the neighbors.

Unfortunately, now that they were both sixteen, Priscilla knew that she'd be seeing more of Susie Byler. There would be volleyball games and singings as well as other youth gatherings. She had even heard a whisper of a camping trip for the youth during June. The boys would go one week on a Thursday and Friday while the girls turn would come on the following Monday and Tuesday. Priscilla wanted very much to attend but she dreaded having to spend so much time with Susie Byler.

Chapter Two

It was Church Sunday. Priscilla was standing with the other young girls, those who had not been baptized yet. The ministers had already walked into the worship room, which was being held in the large open loft that was over the Yoder's horse barn. Soon the older women would walk in, sitting on their side of the room, then the older men. After the married women with small children took their places, their husbands would follow suit. Finally, it would be time for the young, unbaptized youth to enter.

Priscilla felt conscious of the black prayer *kapp* that she wore. Once turned sixteen, she had stopped wearing her white, heart-shaped prayer covering to church and began wearing the black one. It was a symbol that she was over 16 and unmarried. She longed for the day when she would be able to shed her white organdy dress covering and the black prayer *kapp*.

Her eyes trailed the barn to seek out the young men standing along the back wall in the outer room. They would wait until the young women entered before they'd follow. She noticed Stephen Esh standing next to her brothers. At that exact same moment, his eyes seemed to move in her direction and, before she knew it, he was staring at her. The color flooded to her cheeks and she quickly averted her eyes but not before she saw him smile.

"If you think Stephen Esh is interested in taking you home from the singing tonight," someone said softly into her ear. "You're wrong."

Priscilla turned her head, surprised to see Susie Byler standing right behind her. "Whatever are you talking about,

Susie?"

Susie's dark eyes glanced over at Stephen. "I saw you staring at him, Priscilla," Susie said. Her blond hair was pulled back from her face and contrasted sharply against the black prayer *kapp* she wore. She was a pretty girl, despite having such a sharp tongue. But her eyes, so dark and glaring, gave away that there was more to this pretty young woman than her looks. She turned her gaze back to look at Priscilla and frowned. "Quite brazen, if you ask me."

"Sssh," one of the older girls said, casting a stern look at Susie and Priscilla. To be caught talking during church service would certainly warrant unwanted attention and perhaps a lecture from the bishop afterwards. That was something everyone wanted to avoid.

The young girls walked into the room and sat down on the hard benches. The windows were opened and a cool breeze seemed to float through the room. Being that it was early June, the weather was perfect; not too hot or humid yet. White fluffy clouds floated through the sky, which was the bluest of blues that Priscilla could remember. She got lost in the clouds as she gazed out the window, listening to the singing of the Ausbund:

> *The world will persecute you*
> *And inflict much scorn and insult,*
> *Driving out and also freely saying*
> *That Satan is in you.*
>
> *Now when men slander and revile you,*
> *Persecute and beat you for my sake,*
> *Rejoice, for see, your reward*
> *Is prepared for you in Heaven.*[1]

---

[1] Songs of the Ausbund, Song 5 Verse 3-4

She forgot about Susie Byler's nasty accusation earlier and focused on the first minister's sermon. She loved listening to the sing-song lilt of his voice as he preached. There was also so much passion in these sermons. Today, the minister was giving a great discourse about forgiveness and Priscilla tried to absorb everything that he said. He quoted stories from the Bible about Abraham and Jacob. He explained about how Jesus chose to share fellowship with the sinners since they were the ones that needed God's grace the most.

Priscilla watched a few white clouds float across the sky as the minister's sermon sank into her heart. She vowed that she would work harder to forgive others when they disappointed her. It was a hard thing to do, sometimes. She knew that. But she also knew that it was the harder things in life that were usually the most rewarding to achieve.

At the end of the service, Priscilla stood with the rest of the church and faced the outer wall. The men faced one side of the building while the women faced the other. The bishop prayed over the community. Then, as if on silent command, everyone bent down on their knees and cupped their hands against their heads, resting their elbows on the benches where they had previously been seated. For a long time, the church prayed. The prayers were long and silent, deep and private. Priscilla prayed to God to help her learn from the sermon and be able to improve herself as a good Amish Christian woman.

It was during the fellowship hour that she was given her first test. There were to be two seatings for the noon meal that was shared after the service. Sometimes there were even three seatings. It depended on how many visitors attended church.

The young women always took the second seating so that the older men and women as well as the mothers with young children could eat first. During that time, the young women made certain to keep everyone's water glasses filled.

Priscilla stood by the back wall, talking quietly with her friend, Anna Zook. It was her daed's farm that had hosted the service this Sunday. His brother was the bishop so it had been an especially important day for Anna Zook's family.

Both Anna and Priscilla were excited for the singing that was to take place in the evening. After all, Anna whispered, this was their first singing to attend since they had both turned sixteen in the early spring. During the field plowing days of March and April, there weren't many singings. The young men and some of the young women had to get up early in the morning to help their daeds. Priscilla had been one of those young women.

"You two aren't still chattering about tonight's singing, are you?"

Priscilla looked over her shoulder, not surprised to see Susie Byler standing there. "Are you going too, then?" she asked, trying to sound sincere and pleasant. The words of the minister echoed in her head: *Rejoice, for see, your reward is prepared for you in Heaven.*

"Am I going?" Susie sniffed, her tone mocking. "I *have* been going. I've been attending singings for months. In fact, I was attending them last fall!"

Priscilla felt her blood start to boil but she quickly did as her mamm always told her and counted to ten. Twice. What did it matter if Susie had attended singings longer than Priscilla and Anna? Was it that important? After all, Susie had turned sixteen in September while Priscilla had only turned sixteen in May. After the months of plowing and planting, the singings had only started up recently for the upcoming spring, summer, and fall seasons. But she had been unable to attend since her brothers were busy with the fields. It wouldn't have been proper for her to show up without being escorted by one of her brothers.

Trying to find a way to diffuse the unfriendly response from Susie, Priscilla took a deep breath and said, "That's wonderful, Susie. Perhaps you might guide us tonight."

"Guide you?" There was an odd look on her face as if she was stunned at the suggestion. With a flip of her head, she frowned. "Well, I'll just have to pray about that," she said shortly and walked away.

Priscilla stared after her, her mouth almost hanging open. Had Susie really just said that she needed to pray about helping Anna and Priscilla at their first singing? Priscilla had never heard anyone speak to her in such a rude manner. She was unprepared as to how to respond. Clearly this battle with conquering forgiveness was going to be harder than the minister had insinuated.

"Can you believe her?" Anna finally said, her voice barely a whisper.

Oh yes, Priscilla thought. *Forgiveness.* The word echoed in her head. So she merely smiled as she turned to look at her friend. "It's not important, is it? Mayhaps brother Jonas will pick you up tonight when he brings me. That way, we can arrive together. It can't be too hard to attend a singing, now. Can it?"

Anna smiled in appreciation. She didn't have any older

brothers to take her to the singing. All of her brothers were younger. She would have to rely on her younger uncles to take her but many of them didn't live nearby. Having Jonas take her was the perfect solution. "That would sure be nice if you would ask him, Priscilla. You have always been such a good, dear friend."

There was relief in Anna's eyes and Priscilla felt better already. If Susie Byler wasn't going to accept their offer of friendship, it didn't matter. With Anna by her side, Priscilla had all the friendship that she needed. Together, they would attend their first singing and figure it out on their own. They didn't need Susie to guide them. After all, they had each other and that was enough.

Chapter Three

The singing was held in the same room at the Zook farm that had housed the church service earlier in the day. Priscilla and Anna felt giddy and they giggled as they climbed the staircase to the large gathering room. Since it was still sunny outside, the kerosene lanterns that hung from the roof beams hadn't been lit yet. There was a table full of popcorn and pretzels, homemade cookies and pies. Everything looked wunderbaar gut to Priscilla.

Some of the young Amish men lingered nearby, drinking freshly made lemonade and meadow tea while talking. Priscilla was quick to notice that Stephen Esh was at the center of the group. With his brown curly hair and willowy statue, so much taller than most of the other Amish youth, it was hard to miss him. But it was his quick smile and kind blue eyes that always caught her attention. When she walked by, he looked up and smiled at her. Quickly, Priscilla averted her eyes but not before the color rushed to her cheeks.

Anna reached out and touched Priscilla's arm. Thankful for the diversion, Priscilla looked up in time to see her friend motion toward a group of young women standing to the side of the room, near the back window. "Let's go join them," Anna said softly.

They walked over to the window together and stood on the outside of the group. Most of the girls were older, probably eighteen or nineteen. But they all turned and smiled at the newcomers. They remembered what it was like when they first attended a singing.

"It's so nice to see you here," Linda Yoder said, linking

her arm into Priscilla's as they greeted each other.

Priscilla smiled. *"Danke,"* she said, glancing around at the other young women. It was nice to receive such a warm welcome from the older girls and it made her feel less nervous.

"Why, there you are," someone said from the stairwell. Priscilla didn't need to turn around to know who it was. She could tell from the voice that dripped with sugar. "Why Linda Yoder! I am so glad to hear that you're feeling better," Susie said, reaching for Linda's hand, which meant that she needed to release her arm from Priscilla's. Susie casually slid between Linda and Priscilla. "I was thinking about you all week! Summer colds are just the worst!"

Priscilla glanced at Anna but didn't say anything. However, she almost smiled when Anna rolled her eyes. Luckily, no one else saw.

"Danke, Susie. Aren't you so kind?" Linda said softly.

Satisfied, Susie turned around and smiled at another woman. "And Rachel! I saw your new quilt hanging in the shop in Intercourse. I think you have the finest stitches I've ever seen! And that pattern! Wherever did you come up with it?"

"It was my grandmother's," Rachel said, beaming from the praise.

The praise continued around the small circle, Susie finding something to say to each woman that brought a wide smile to their faces. However, her praise stopped short when she saw Priscilla and Anna standing nearby. She met their gaze and frowned before turning back to the older young women. "I think I'll get some refreshments before the singing starts," she said, turning her attention back to the other young women. "Linda, would you like something?"

Several of the other women walked with Susie over to the table, leaving Anna and Priscilla standing to the side, alone and feeling lost. They stared after Susie who had quickly made herself the center of attention by praising the other girls and asking them lots of questions. But she hadn't even said so much as hello to Priscilla or Anna.

"Oh, she makes me think terrible things," Priscilla mumbled. She hated to admit it but it was true. It wasn't that she wanted to be the center of attention but she certainly didn't want to be made to feel like an outsider.

"I know," Anna sighed. "Just keep thinking about today's sermon."

"I am," Priscilla whispered. *Forgiveness,* she repeated to herself. "It's what is keeping my words in my head and not on my lips."

The singing began a short time later. Anna and Priscilla sat in the second row of benches with the other young women. Priscilla loved listening to the songs, each one begun by one of the young men who would sing the first word of the hymn before the rest of the group joined in the song. The hymns were sung faster than the ones during the church service. Priscilla had never heard the hymns sung in a faster manner and the sound fascinated her. It was beautiful music and the words touched her heart. Once again, she vowed to keep her patience in check when it came to that Susie Byler.

When the group broke for refreshments, Jonas came over to Anna and Priscilla carrying two cups of lemonade. He smiled at his sister, pleased to see that she was fitting in without his help. "You like the singing, then, ja?" he asked.

Priscilla nodded her head. "It's so beautiful. I love the

music and the songs; so different than at church."

Her brother smiled at his youngest sister. He had always been protective and caring of her. They had a special bond from being so close in age, but also due to his tender nature. "*Das ist gut,*" he said and glanced at Anna. He gave her a friendly smile as he handed her the cup of lemonade. "And you?"

Anna was quick to reply. "I feel so grown up!"

Jonas laughed. "Well," he replied, a sparkle in his blue eyes, "You are sixteen now. Mayhaps you'll get an invitation to ride home in a buggy with someone."

She flushed.

"If not, you'll just be stuck with me," he added and grinned.

Priscilla looked up, realizing that Jonas was, indeed, stuck with bringing both her and Anna home. She hadn't realized that when she had asked him to pick up Anna. Now, if there was a young lady he wanted to bring home, he couldn't. "Oh Jonas," she gasped. "We can always walk home. I didn't think..." This was, after all, his time of courting, too.

He placed a hand on her arm to stop her. "Mayhaps I'd prefer nothing more than to take you both home." And she could tell from his expression that he was sincere. He straightened his back and glanced around. "Two prettiest girls here, anyway," he teased. "And the nicest! There's no one else I'd like to ask to ride home with me anyway!"

Both Anna and Priscilla lowered their eyes and the color rushed to their cheeks. Even if Jonas was being brotherly, compliments were far and few between. He laughed at their modesty and winked at Anna before he hurried back to his group of friends before the next round of songs began. For a split second, Priscilla wondered about that twinkle in his eye when he had looked at Anna. Could he have been telling the truth that there was no one else he'd like to ride home with after the singing?

It was after the second set of songs that Priscilla excused herself to visit the restroom. It was getting warm in the room and she wanted to put some cool water on the back of her neck. The evening had been exciting and new, something different for Priscilla. Besides the faster, new hymns that were sung, some of the young men told funny jokes and stories between the songs. There was a lot of laughter among the young people. Priscilla was enjoying herself so much that she wished it didn't have to end. After all, it would be two more weeks until the next singing.

"Priscilla Smucker," a voice said as she walked out of the restroom. Turning at the sounds, she was surprised to see Stephen Esh standing there. He was leaning against the wall, tucked behind a pillar so that prying eyes couldn't see him. She wondered if he had been waiting to use the restroom or had been waiting for her. With his thick shock of curly brown hair and big blue eyes, it was always hard to miss Stephen Esh, even if he wasn't so tall. "I was looking for you," he added.

Looking for her? Priscilla frowned. Why on earth would Stephen Esh be looking for her? "Whatever for?" she asked, immediately hating the way that sounded and wishing she could gobble the words right back up.

He laughed and moved closer to her. With a quick glance over his shoulder to make certain no one was listening, he leaned down. He was so close that she could smell the fresh scent of lavender on his skin. It was a fresh smell and she caught her breath when he lowered his voice and said, "I know tonight is your first singing, Priscilla."

She wondered why he would care about tonight being her first singing. She had rarely ever talked to him. He was older and, even in school, he ran with the boys that were the age of her older brother, David. "Yes it is," she finally said, trying to still her beating heart.

He straightened his back and took a deep breath. Suddenly, he seemed very serious. "I was hoping I could take you home tonight."

Priscilla felt her heart flip-flop inside of her chest. She knew that this was the time for the young men to get to know the young women. It would start with a buggy ride home after the singings. Then it would be buggy rides home after volleyball games. Eventually, if the rides continued and compatibility was apparent, the young man might even ask to pick her up to take her to these social events. But Stephen Esh was asking her!

From what she had heard, Stephen Esh was not one to ask girls to ride home, at least not just one. He might take two girls home, but he always seemed to avoid being linked romantically with anyone. That had seemed to get the attention of more than one young woman who had hoped to be the first to capture his interest and affection.

Priscilla, however, had been so excited to go to her first singing that she had never given much thought to being asked home. Usually the younger women would walk home or ride home with their brothers. She certainly had never thought that Stephen Esh would single her out.

"Oh," she said softly. She was too surprised to think

straight.

"Is that a yes or a no?" he whispered, his breath warm on her cheek.

"I...I..." She didn't know how to respond. No one had prepared her for this type of situation. Finally, she took a deep breath and looked up, meeting his eyes. "That would be right gut, Stephen. I think I should like that."

"*Wunderbaar!*" He smiled. "Don't you forget that you promised me and let another man ask you home," he said, his eyes twinkling. He touched her arm gently, a friendly and reassuring gesture, before he quickly moved away, rejoining his friends before they would begin to ask questions about his disappearance.

A stunned Priscilla stood there for a moment, trying to recapture what had just happened. A first buggy ride was a big moment. She hadn't expected that tonight. Indeed, she was too focused on the experience. She knew that, one day, someone would ask her home. But on her first singing? And to be asked by Stephen Esh of all people!

Most women didn't talk about their courtships. But Priscilla did know that the buggy rides were important. It was a time to get to know each other privately. Once a young girl turned sixteen, they were free to court young men. While it didn't happen too often, some girls even got married at eighteen. But it always started with a buggy ride. If he asked her again, after tonight, that would mean he was interested in courting her.

He was so well thought of in the community! At twenty-one, he was older than some of the other young men at the singing. He had already bought a small farm down the road from his daed's farm. While he still lived at home with his parents, he worked that farm harder than anyone else. He'd help his daed with his own chores before hurrying down the road to plow his fields and plant his crops. The entire church district was impressed with his hard work and willingness to help others.

She sat back onto the bench next to Anna and reached for her friend's hand. Giving it a squeeze, she whispered into Anna's ear, "You're never going to believe what just happened..."

Chapter Four

The following morning, Priscilla woke up early, with a warm and tingly feeling inside her. She shut her eyes and tried to remember every detail of that wonderful buggy ride home. He had waited for her by the staircase and motioned to her when no one was looking. Riding home from the singings was a private matter, not one for the public to talk about, especially at the early stages of courtship. This saved both parties from any possible embarrassment should the courtship not progress further. For that, Priscilla was thankful.

She had followed him down the stairs and outside to where his buggy was waiting. He had opened the door for her and helped her inside, his hand gently holding her arm, even though she didn't really need his assistance. When he was inside the buggy and had slid the buggy's door so that it was closed, he turned and smiled at her. "Comfortable?" he had asked.

She was surprised. He had seemed to be nervous when, in reality, it was her stomach that was filled with butterflies. She couldn't imagine what he had to be nervous about, after all. Wasn't it Stephen who had asked her to ride home with him? "Ja," she replied. Satisfied with her answer, he had released the brake and urged his horse forward and down the lane.

For a few minutes, neither one of them exchanged words. Priscilla had clutched her hands on her lap, wringing them nervously. She didn't know whether she was supposed to ask him questions or if he was supposed to be the one to initiate conversation. She had finally decided to let him take charge. After all, he was five years older than her and would think her far too forward if she spoke first.

Once the horse was trotting down the road, further from the singing, he seemed to relax. He slowed the horse down and, when it came time to take a right at the fork in the road, she noticed that Stephen turned left. She was about to correct him but she stopped herself. Stephen certainly knew where she lived and must have his own reasons for taking the longer route.

"You enjoyed your first singing?" he had asked, finally breaking the silence.

"Oh yes," she gushed, happy for his question. The silence had been too awkward. Having something to talk about was much better. "It was wunderbaar gut."

He nodded his head. "Ja, nice to have some social time with friends, ain't so?"

"It was so very nice," she admitted.

"You turned sixteen when?" he asked.

"Back in May but we didn't have singings then," she responded, wondering why he was curious about her birth month.

"You sure have a pretty singing voice," he said. She was thankful that it was dark in the buggy for, otherwise, he would have seen her blush.

With the ice broken, they had talked for the next hour as Stephen guided his horse down some back roads. Priscilla forgot that they were on the way to her daed's farm. Instead, she became absorbed in his stories about working his own farm, helping his daed, and some of the funny stories about his sibblings. As the oldest son of ten, Stephen had a different perspective on family than Priscilla did. After all, she was the youngest of eight children.

When he had finally stopped the buggy in her daed's driveway, he waited a few seconds before sliding open the buggy door. Holding the reins in his hands, he seemed to be contemplating something. Priscilla wasn't certain what she was supposed to do so she waited. Clearly, Stephen had done this before and, knowing that she hadn't, he would know how the buggy ride was supposed to end.

"There's a volleyball game next Saturday evening," he had finally said. "I know that Jonas usually attends and I reckon you'll be going with him, ja?"

Priscilla had raised her eyebrows, wondering why he was asking her such a question. "I hadn't heard about it. I suppose if he goes and asks me, I would go along. Where is it taking place?"

"At the Yoders," he had said. "Ja, vell..." he hesitated. There was a catch in his voice and he cleared his throat. "Mayhaps you'd let me bring you home again, afterwards?"

For the second time that evening, she had caught her breath. Could it be possible, she had wondered, that Stephen Esh was, indeed, interested in her? They had known each other for all of their lives but, because he was older, she hadn't ever spent time with him. She knew that he was friendly with her older brother David since they were just one year apart in age. But Stephen Esh had always seemed to be so much more mature and focused on his farming. At church services, there were many eyes of Amish young women that wandered in his direction, especially when the sermons were too long and uninteresting.

Now, Stephen Esh was asking her to ride home with him

after the volleyball game? "Oh," she started breathlessly. "That would be just fine, Stephen."

He seemed to smile, she sensed, but she wasn't certain for it was dark in the buggy. But she could tell that he was more relaxed. "Gut!" he had said, his voice sounding definitely more enthusiastic. "I will see you then." With that, he had slid open the door, jumped down to the driveway and reached inside to take her hand and help her out.

Now, the morning after, Priscilla couldn't help but smile to herself. Stephen Esh was, indeed, interested in getting to know her better. If she had thought he had just been nice to ask her home so that she would have a lovely memory of her first singing, she now knew for a fact that she might very well be on the way to her first courtship. First courtship, she thought with a smile. Would it possibly also be her last?

Without any question, Priscilla knew that a match with Samuel Esh would be a good one. He'd be a wunderbaar provider and, after having helped his parents with his nine brothers and sisters, he'd be an even better daed. Any girl would be lucky to have captured his attention. Priscilla just couldn't figure out why she was one of them.

Downstairs, her mamm was already busy at the stove, cooking breakfast for the men who were outside milking the cows and tending to the horses and mules. Mamm looked over her shoulder and smiled as Priscilla entered the room from the stairwell.

"My, my," her mamm teased. Her arms were covered in flour and she was busy kneading a loaf of bread. Mondays, Wednesdays, and Fridays were bread making days in the Smucker house. "Good ... afternoon!"

Priscilla pretended to frown at her mamm. "It's only six!"

"Ja, but I've been up since five!" Her mamm raised a delicate eyebrow. "Must have been home awfully late from that singing to sleep in an extra hour on a Monday! Let's not forget that today is wash day after all." But Priscilla could tell that her mamm was not really upset with her. No, indeed, her mamm was her best friend. However, even though they were very close, her mamm knew better than to probe about who had actually brought her home the evening before, despite making it clear that she was aware it wasn't her brother.

By seven o'clock, the bread was rising on the counter and the table was set. Steaming bowls of scrambled eggs, home-made granola, fresh bread, and scrapple were waiting for the men. Once everyone had sat down at the table and bowed their heads for the before-meal prayer, the plates were passed and conversation started to flow.

"Have a surprise for you, Priscilla," Jonas said, looking up from his food.

"Me?" she asked, her voice squeaking.

"Ja! I was talking last night with Polly Yoder. She's coordinating the charity event at the Mennonite church in July. I told her that you'd be entering some of your tomatoes. They'll be part of the donation auction to raise money for the needy."

The rest of the room fell silent. No one spoke as all eyes turned to Priscilla. Even her daed sat motionless, his eyebrows raised in surprise and his fork stopped midway between his plate and mouth. It was unlike Jonas to pay such particular interest in something that was traditionally not of interest to men. Donating goods to a charity auction was something that their mamm would have arranged, not her brother.

"Jonas!" Priscilla gasped. "Why on earth...?"

Her mamm bit her lip and turned her eyes toward her son. "I would like to think that you would have discussed it with your sister first."

Jonas rolled his eyes. "Oh mamm, you know how modest she is. She'd never have entered such an event!"

David laughed.

Priscilla was still stunned and could barely speak.

Mamm turned her attention back to Priscilla. "What do you think about that, daughter? I'm sure Polly Yoder would understand if you told her that Jonas spoke up for you without permission."

Jonas was quick to jump back into the discussion. "No," he said. "You best not do that."

"Why ever not?" Priscilla finally said, her heart pounding inside of her chest. Would the rest of the Amish youth in her district think that she was proud? She didn't like being in the spotlight.

Again, David laughed. "Bet I know why."

Jonas glared at him. It was suddenly quite obvious that there was more to the matter than Jonas having a kind heart and wanting to help the needy. With a sigh, he finally admitted, "It's that Susie Byler."

This time, it was their daed who laughed. His eyes crinkled and he set his fork down on his plate. Wiping at his mouth with a napkin, he shook his head, still smiling. "Not that Jacob's daughter again."

With a frown on his face, Jonas seemed disgusted. "I couldn't help myself. She is too proud and was reminding everyone last night how she had the biggest tomatoes and her bushel had bought in the most donations last year. She says that she has a secret way to plant and garden and that no one else knows it."

Mamm took a deep breath. "I'm not liking what I'm hearing about this child. She sure does seem too proud."

"Well," Jonas continued. "I couldn't stop myself. When I heard the bragging, I mentioned to Polly that Priscilla would be donating her own tomatoes to the charity. You should have seen that Susie's face. When the attention turned from her to Priscilla, she turned as red as..."

"A tomato?" David finished the sentence for him.

Everyone laughed at the joke, everyone except Priscilla and Mamm.

"Oh boys," Mamm said, trying to remain somber. "We should pray for that girl instead of instigate her. Challenging her in a competition is not very kind, is it now?" Jonas and David lowered their heads. But Priscilla could tell from their expressions that they weren't sorry in the least bit.

Her mamm turned her attention to her. "Priscilla," her mamm continued gently. "It's up to you if you wish to donate the tomatoes. But do it for the right reasons. Any money brought in will help the Mennonites with their work of helping those that are less fortunate. That," she said, looking sternly at her two sons. "Is a good reason to enter the contest, not to have bragging rights over how much money is raised or to show up a prideful young woman."

A silence fell over the table and Priscilla chewed on her

lower lip. The thought of listening to Susie Byler for the next few weeks and for months afterward did not interest Priscilla at all. She also knew that if Susie found out that Stephen Esh had showed an interest in her, that would raise more problems with Susie who had been adamant that Priscilla would not be riding in a buggy with him. She wanted to avoid any further upset with Susie, that was for sure and certain.

However, her mamm had a good point. Any money raised from her donation would help the less fortunate. If her tomatoes could help raise money, that was a very good cause. Not donating them to avoid listening to Susie was just as bad as being prideful. Besides, she thought, Jonas volunteered me. No one can claim that I'm the proud one in the charity drive.

"I'll do it," she said, ignoring the look of victory on Jonas's face. "But only because it may help those in need."

Chapter Five

For the next few days, Priscilla seemed to forget about the charity day. After all, it was still weeks away. She did her chores in the house, helped her daed and brothers with cutting hay, and even helped with baling it. Then, in the late afternoons, when her brothers were milking the cows, she would tend to her garden.

This was her favorite time of day. The late afternoon breeze was cool, the birds were singing and she could hear the cows in the dairy barn. All thoughts of the charity drive and Susie Byler were far from her mind. But one thing was never far from it: Stephen Esh. She counted down the days until Saturday evening.

Since this weekend was an off-Sunday, there would not be a singing. The Amish youth only held singings in the evenings after church service. On those weekends when there was no singing, many of the youth gathered for volleyball games at a farm in the district. Sometimes other district youth joined. But Priscilla didn't care about that since she already knew that she'd be riding home with Stephen Esh. She didn't have to think about anything else except those long minutes, alone in the buggy, talking with Stephen.

When she worked in the garden, she used her hoe to dig up the earth and pull out the weeds. She tended to the tomato plants with as much care as she could. She always broke off the bottom branches so that the good, healthy nutrients could focus on the top of the tomato bush. That was where the juiciest tomatoes would grow. Sometimes, she even talked to the plants, thanking them for giving the family such a bounty of food.

By Saturday, Priscilla was anxious for the volleyball game. After all, this was another first for her. She had never attended one as a sixteen year old. Her brother Jonas laughed at her as she smoothed back her hair just one more time in the small mirror that hung over the sink in the utility room.

"If you keep looking in that mirror, you might start seeing some gray hairs pop out," he teased.

Priscilla frowned and looked over her shoulder at him. "You'll be nice to me, Jonas," she said. "I bet you were the same way when you first went to a Saturday evening social gathering!"

Her mamm finished wiping down the counter. They had eaten a light supper at five, just before the evening milking. Luckily, Daed and David had volunteered to milk the cows so that Jonas could get ready and take Priscilla to the volleyball game. "Ja, he sure was," Mamm chimed in. "Dusted his boots until they shone so much that he didn't need a mirror to see *his* reflection."

Jonas had offered to pick up Anna so they left earlier to travel the extra miles to her daed's farm. She smiled as she jumped into the buggy, sitting beside Priscilla in the front, her body hanging partially out of the door. It was cooler and a lot of the youths liked to ride that way, despite the bishop reprimanding them for it being dangerous.

When they arrived at the Yoder's farm, Priscilla and Anna noticed that most of the youth from their district were already there, along with some others that they had not met before. They noticed Polly and Sarah standing in the group so they hurried over to join them, hoping to get to know the other young women a bit better. Since they were older, neither Priscilla nor Anna had much opportunity to know them outside of the fellowship time following services on Church Sundays. This was the perfect opportunity to correct that.

However, Priscilla's heart skipped a beat when she saw that Susie Byler was already in the middle of the circle, giving her usual round of praise to everyone that was listening. She had some comment to give to everyone, some compliment or question. Priscilla quickly noticed that, despite the appearance of interest in the other women, everything eventually seemed to return to focus on Susie. Standing on the outside of the group, it was easy to see that Susie was trying to control the other girls and win their favors with overly abundant compliments. Clearly, she wanted to be the center of attention and affection in the group.

Priscilla started to turn around and walk away, disgusted with what was so obvious to her yet so unapparent to the others. She didn't like the un-Amish-like manner in which Susie Byler behaved. Rather than be exposed as having negative feelings toward another, Priscilla preferred to find somewhere else to stand.

Unfortunately, Polly saw her turn to go and interrupted Susie's latest story about her wonderful gardening skills.

"Priscilla Smucker!" Polly called out. All of the young women turned to look at Priscilla. "Come back here and tell us about your garden." Polly smiled and waved her hand. "Your brother said you are going to donate tomatoes to the charity dinner. He said you raise wonderful beefsteak tomatoes."

Priscilla flushed and paused, not liking the attention. She was not used to people singling her out and she felt most uncomfortable. Yet, everyone was staring at her and waiting for a response. As she glanced at them, trying to figure out how to respond, she noticed that Susie Byler was glaring in her direction. Her dark eyes flashed with anger but no one else seemed to notice. Turning her attention back to Polly, Priscilla nodded her head. "Ja, brother Jonas told me that he had volunteered my donation," she said. "After talking it over with my mamm, we felt that it was a right gut thing to do since it will raise money to help those in need."

The other girls smiled and nodded their heads. Sarah Lapp reached her hand out and touched Priscilla's arm. "You are such a good person, Priscilla. Always been so sweet and thoughtful. We should all do the same as you...donate something to help those in need."

Priscilla noticed that everyone nodded and quickly began volunteering to donate canned goods and meats, loaves of fresh bread and pies. The more people started clamoring around Priscilla and Polly, focusing on the community effort for the charity dinner, the darker Susie Byler's face became. It was as if a dark cloud had passed over it and Priscilla felt a deep fear growing inside of her. She had never seen such ugliness manifest itself in someone's expression and she certainly had never wanted to see such anger pointed in her direction.

During the volleyball game, Priscilla tried to forget about the uneasy feeling she had felt earlier. She played the volleyball game, laughing with Anna, Polly, and Sarah, despite feeling heat from Susie's glares on the back of her neck. Then, when Stephen Esh caught up with her between games, bringing her a cup of fresh meadow tea, Priscilla found herself focusing on something new: The way that Stephen had smiled at her.

So it caught her off-guard when she heard a whisper in her ear. "It recently came to my attention," the voice hissed. "That you are copying my gardening secrets."

Priscilla turned around, startled by the voice and the accusation. "Whatever are you talking about, Susie Byler?"

Susie put her hand on her hip. Her dark eyes flashed and a strand of her very blond hair fell out from under her prayer *kapp*. "I know that you copy my pattern of how to grow tomatoes in the tomato patch! You also use store-bought fertilizer instead of natural fertilizer because you want the biggest tomatoes!"

Priscilla frowned. "That is most certainly not true! I have never even seen your garden!"

Susie snorted. "You can pretend not to know but I know the truth." She lowered her voice, her eyes piercing as she glared at Priscilla. "I heard about you donating food to the charity dinner. I make it my business to know these things, you see. You think you are so smart but you are no more than a copycat. Several other people have noticed this, too. They are all talking about it." She paused. "They are all talking about you and what a liar you are."

Priscilla started to say something but Susie put up her hand to stop her. It was a rude gesture and Priscilla was caught off-guard.

"I raised the most money last year with my tomatoes because I know how to grow the best tomatoes," Susie stated, her hands on her hips. "I would think that you'd want your tomatoes to stand on their own merit. Instead, they will just think you are mimicking me."

Priscilla took a deep breath, wishing that someone was

around to overhear this discussion. But they were alone. "Since you already grow the best tomatoes, I reckon you have nothing to worry about. Besides, I'm growing the tomatoes to help raise money for the needy, not to be recognized as the best."

Susie glared again and leaned forward, her face just inches from Priscilla's. "I'm going to tell you something right now, Priscilla Smucker. If, and when, I find out that you copied me, I'm going to complain to the bishop. You will be removed from the charity drive and everyone will know that you are a liar."

For a moment, Priscilla was speechless. The attack was completely unprovoked on her part. The accusations were beyond ridiculous. Yet, there was nothing she could do about it. "You are absolutely crazy," she whispered. "Don't talk to me anymore."

"Oh," Susie said, a sneer on her face. "If I'm crazy, I can't help it. But you...you with your lying serpent's tongue...you can." And Susie turned on her heel and stormed away, her expression suddenly returned to normal as she rejoined the volleyball game and began laughing with her friends.

Priscilla stood there, her mouth hanging open and her heart heavy in her chest. She felt tears well up into the corners of her eyes and she had to reach up to wipe them away. She couldn't go back to the volleyball game, not the way she was feeling. Her hands were shaking, her heart was racing and her stomach was twisted in a knot. This was all so unfair and uncalled for.

She was still standing there when Stephen Esh came over to see what was wrong, Priscilla knew better than to confide in him. It would be wrong to tell someone what Susie had just said for that might be construed as gossip. And she knew that no one liked a gossip. So, instead, she tried to smile but she knew that she was still tense and upset.

This time, on the buggy ride home, Priscilla didn't feel so talkative. She was still in turmoil over the disturbing things that Susie Byler had accused her of. Her stomach felt thick and heavy as if she had a pit inside there that churned. She even felt the beginning of a headache, although she couldn't be sure if it was from the warm evening air or the stress of the unprovoked confrontation with Susie.

During the buggy ride, Stephen had asked her a few questions but Priscilla was so distracted by her own thoughts about that horrible conversation with Susie that twice she had to ask him to repeat the question. Her distraction was too apparent and, eventually, he stopped asking her questions. They rode home in silence and, when he dropped her off, he did not ask her to ride home with him from future events.

"How was the volleyball game?" her mamm asked when she walked into the kitchen. Her mamm was sitting on the rocking chair, stitching at a quilt square.

Priscilla hesitated, wanting to talk to her mamm but not wanting to upset her. There would be too many questions and, by speaking with her mamm about what was going on, her mamm might force her to go to the bishop. That would certainly set off a string of additional issues. The last thing that Priscilla wanted to do was to make Susie Byler look bad in the eyes of the community.

"It was fine," she responded. But she knew that her voice wasn't very convincing by the way her mamm raised an eyebrow and watched her hurry up the stairs.

When she plopped onto her bed and buried her face into her pillow, she cried. How could Susie Byler ruin what had the potential to be a wonderful evening? Because of that horrid young woman, Stephen would certainly never ask her to go riding again. All because of tomatoes!

She felt like her entire world had just collapsed and there simply wasn't one thing that she could do about it. She had never felt so helpless in her life.

Chapter Six

It was Anna who brought the subject up to Priscilla the following Wednesday. Despite living almost two miles away, Anna had ridden her scooter over to the Smucker farm, a concerned look on her face. She found Priscilla in the garden, working on the tomato plants. Anna set her scooter down on the driveway and hurried across the grass.

"You're never going to believe this," Anna said as she approached.

Priscilla could sense the urgency in Anna's voice and set the hoe on the ground, careful not to crush any plants. It wasn't like Anna to stop by in the middle of the afternoon. And she looked so distraught. Clearly, something was bothering her. "What's wrong, Anna?"

"I just had the most disturbing conversation with that Susie Byler yesterday," Anna said. Her face was pale and her brown eyes large. "I'm still shaking."

"Oh dear," Priscilla said. She didn't have to hear the details for she was fairly certain that she knew exactly what Anna was going to say. "Let me guess...it's about the charity dinner."

Anna looked up, her eyes wide and surprised. "How did you know?"

Priscilla quickly told her about the conversation from the volleyball game. "I'm telling you, I've never seen such a look on anyone's face," Priscilla said when she finished her story. "I was actually scared."

Nodding her head, Anna admitted the same. "She's not

right, I'm afraid. Something is definitely wrong. I heard that she just works in her garden all day, only stops to eat and eventually sleep. Her daed doesn't need her help in the fields and her mamm wants her to be happy. They don't even see that something is wrong with her."

"Do you think that she's obsessed with this charity dinner?" Priscilla gasped.

Anna nodded. "I'm starting to think that very same thing. The more anyone seems to talk about other people donating vegetables to the charity, the angrier she seems to get." Anna lowered her voice, even though no one else was around. "I think she is jealous when other people get any attention."

That didn't sound right to Priscilla. Amish were taught to help and support each other. Jealousy was not something that reared its ugly head within the district too often. In fact, modesty was a highly valued characteristic in an Amish woman. If Susie Byler was, indeed, jealous, she was prideful and that could very well hinder her from ever getting appreciated within the community. "She needs help," Priscilla said.

Anna frowned. "I'm not about to tell her that. Not the way that she spoke to me."

"No, no," Priscilla agreed. She had made it clear that she didn't want to speak with Susie Byler again. "But she's obviously got issues. Mayhaps the bishop could talk to her."

Anna sighed. "This is all so silly, isn't it?"

Priscilla nodded. Anna was right. The whole situation was almost comical...if only it wasn't really happening. "I have been so upset about it. Would it be awful to admit that I feel a little bit better to know that she's after you, too?"

Anna laughed. "I suppose I can understand that. I guess we are just the newcomers to the group and she must feel a bit threatened, ain't so?"

"Ain't so, indeed!" Priscilla joined Anna in laughing at the situation. But it wasn't an honest laugh. Instead, it was full of sadness and regret. She was worried about the upcoming singing. Would Stephen Esh ask to bring her home again? She doubted it. Not after the way she behaved after the volleyball game. Certainly he would think she wasn't interested or simply dull. Just one more thing that Susie Byler had ruined, she thought angrily.

She spent the best part of the next few days quietly reflecting on the situation and hoping that it would die down. After all, the charity dinner was only one week away now. Priscilla couldn't imagine that it could get any worse.

On the Sunday after the service, she realized that she had been wrong. She had sat next to several of the girls during the service and noticed that they were behaving strangely toward her. One of them seemed to lean away from Priscilla and no one whispered to her during the sermon. Their behavior was indeed peculiar. At first, Priscilla didn't find that strange, especially since Bishop Zook was preaching today. No one whispered when the bishop drew the lot to preach.

But afterwards, it was Sarah Lapp who pulled Priscilla aside. Grabbing her hand, she took Priscilla out of the barn where the service had been held and they walked around the corner where no one was standing. She looked pale and unnerved. Without hearing a word, Priscilla knew exactly why Sarah was looking so unhappy and a pit quickly formed in her stomach.

Yet, she wasn't prepared for Sarah's first question. "Did you destroy some of Susie Byler's tomatoes?"

"What?" Priscilla said, her heart beginning to pound inside of her chest. She could barely believe that Sarah had asked her that question. She repeated it in her mind, trying to decide whether or not she had misheard what Sarah had actually said. "What are you talking about?"

Sarah nodded her head. "You heard me right. Susie Byler was telling Polly and some of the other girls that you went to her house and crushed some of her tomato plants last night."

The tears began to well up in Priscilla's eyes. What a vile accusation, she thought. "That's not true at all! How could she say that?"

"I know, Priscilla," Sarah said, reaching out to rub Priscilla's arm to comfort her. "But I wanted you to know what she's saying."

Priscilla felt sick to her stomach. How could anyone say such a thing? Then, it dawned on her that Sarah had asked her for a reason. "Are people believing her?"

Sarah nodded again. "Some are, yes."

Priscilla let out a sob as she lifted her hand to her cover her mouth. How could anyone believe such a horrid lie? No one in their community would do something so dreadful. Vandalize another person's property? To state something like that was just despicable and Priscilla was stunned. "That's an outright lie," she said, wiping the tears that fell down her cheeks.

"It gets worse," Sarah said. "She even went so far as to demand that Polly not let you participate in the charity dinner."

"Can she do that?" Priscilla gasped. After all of her hard work, was it possible that now, because of Susie Byler, she couldn't donate her tomatoes to help raise money for charity? "Why is Susie doing this?"

Sarah frowned and shook her head. "She's jealous, Priscilla. Think about it. She won last year, received all of the attention from everyone at the singings and social events, and then you showed up with Anna. She didn't like the idea of having competition. It took away from her own glory."

"But she's not going after you or Polly or any of the other girls!"

Sarah shrugged. "She's younger than them. Wouldn't make sense to attack them, I reckon."

"This is terrible," Priscilla moaned. She had never been the subject of such bullying before. In fact, she had never heard of anyone being bullied in their community. Of course, there was that issue in Ohio of the renegade Amish man who bullied people in his community for having different beliefs. But that was so far away and had resulted in some physical attacks, not social or emotional. No one in Priscilla's family had ever talked about how to handle such situations. "What do I do?"

Sarah smiled but there was sorrow in her eyes. "You keep working on your tomatoes and you donate them to that dinner."

Priscilla frowned. "But I thought you said Susie wanted me thrown out of the charity event. I thought Polly was going to tell me to..."

Holding up a hand, Sarah stopped Priscilla in midstream. "Do you think that Polly Yoder would let Susie Byler bully her? In fact, she gave Susie the what-for, Priscilla.

She still wants you to donate your tomatoes and refuses to listen to Susie Byler, even if Susie is now telling the other girls that Polly is taking your side."

"Oh Sarah," Priscilla said through her tears. "I'm ever so glad you told me that. It means so much to know that you believe me."

This time, Sarah leaned forward and hugged Priscilla. "Never you mind," she said when she pulled back. "I was nice to her even though I could see through her false praise of everyone and everything. But I won't let her try to make me do something that I don't want to do and I sure won't believe that you, Priscilla Smucker, would ever try to sabotage another gardener...or anyone for that matter."

Later that night, when Jonas knocked at her bedroom door and asked if she was ready to go to the singing, Priscilla opened the door and peeked out. She hadn't planned to go to the singing, not now that she knew people were talking about her and thinking such horrible things. All of her life, she had tried to do the right thing and help others. To know that some of the people she had considered friends believed Susie's outrageous lies upset her. But she didn't want to tell her brother what was being said.

"I don't feel so well," she whispered through the crack in the door. It was the truth. Her stomach was in a knot and she didn't want to leave the house.

He frowned. "Nonsense."

"I don't..."

He wedged his foot in the door so that she couldn't shut it. "You get yourself ready, Priscilla Smucker. I know darn well what's going on with that nasty Susie Byler. Your true friends know you didn't do what she said. You aren't a copycat or a liar. And, for sure and certain, you didn't destroy any of her silly tomato plants."

Priscilla gasped, swinging the door wide open. "You know about that?" She wondered if the word had reached her mamm and daed? If so, they hadn't spoken to her about it. She reckoned they were just going to let her handle it herself.

Jonas rolled his eyes. "I make it my business to look out for you, sister." He leaned against the doorframe and smiled at her. "Now, you get ready and let's go. Don't give that crazy woman the satisfaction of thinking she won."

Taking a deep breath, Priscilla knew that he was right. If she were to hide from Susie Byler and any of those false friends who believed Susie instead of asking Priscilla what had really happened, then Susie Byler would have gotten her way. Rewarding her lies and deceitful nature was not something that Priscilla wanted to do. Plus, she thought, I have nothing to hide.

Chapter Seven

The singing was held in a barn that evening. It was cooler as a rainstorm had swept through Ephrata earlier in the day. Priscilla kept to herself at the back of the barn, watching the other girls and wondering whom among them was listening to and, even worse, believing Susie Byler and her horrible lies. She felt so unprotected and vulnerable, but she tried to keep a happy face, knowing that she had done absolutely nothing to provoke the wrath of Susie.

She noticed that a few of the girls glanced at her over their shoulders then looked away when Priscilla noticed them. It hurt Priscilla to know that people she had once thought were her friends were, in reality, not. She wondered what the bishop would say about such behavior. It certainly wasn't what the Amish people typically practiced. With a sigh, Priscilla straightened her back and dipped her head to look at the hymnal rather than focus on the stares of the girls or the heaviness of her heart.

"She's really going after Polly now," Sarah whispered in her ear. "Since you've been avoiding her, she's really creating a stir that Polly is favoring your donation, even though you supposedly crushed her tomatoes."

Priscilla sighed. "That's just ridiculous. Why would I do something like that?"

"So she couldn't enter," Sarah said. "But I have to tell you that I had been at her farm the day before and she was showing me her garden. That tomato patch was riddled with signs of bugs. I think her tomatoes just weren't good enough to enter in a charity event and she knew it!"

Priscilla caught her breath. "Are you saying that she might have crushed those plants herself and blamed me for it?"

With a casual lifting of her eyebrow, Sarah shrugged. "Who knows? The way that she is behaving is strange enough, don't you think?"

"I just don't believe it," Priscilla mumbled to herself. Was it possible that Susie would destroy her own property to blame Priscilla for it? And why was Susie so determined to ruin Priscilla's reputation? They had never had any exchanges before the other week. In fact, she lived on the furthest side of the district from the Smucker farm. They practically had no interactions whatsoever. So Susie's determination to make people think poorly of her was even more concerning. Priscilla had never experienced such a situation. It was upsetting to her, for sure and certain.

During the first break, she was about to slip out the door and walk home by herself. She had enough of feeling uncomfortable. Between the pit in her stomach and the worry over who was talking about her, she wanted nothing more than to leave. It had been a mistake to let Jonas talk her into attending the singing. She should have stayed home and let this entire situation fade away.

The gentle tug on her arm surprised her and she turned around, finding herself staring up at Stephen Esh. His eyes twinkled at her. "You ran out so fast after the church service," he said, leaning over so that his voice was a soft breath against her ear. "I was afraid you were feeling poorly and wouldn't come tonight."

"Oh no," she said. "I..." She wasn't certain how to explain it. Could the horrible stories that Susie Byler was spreading have escaped his ears? Or did he know and simply did not believe Susie? The conflicting thoughts worried her and she wasn't certain of what to say. "I needed some time to think. I have a little thorn in my side and I wanted to sort some things through."

Stephen laughed softly. "Oh don't you worry about that thorn, Priscilla. People who know you," he said. "Well, they know the difference between truth and jealousy." He smiled at her and his eyes seemed to soften when he did so.

She felt a wave of relief wash over her. So he knew and didn't believe? For a moment, she didn't care about Susie Byler anymore. Stephen Esh had enough faith in her to not believe Susie's lies.

He reached out and touched her arm. "Is that why you were so unhappy the other week on the buggy ride home?"

She jumped at his touch. It was so soft and gentle, a gesture of intimacy that surprised her. But she didn't say anything as she hesitated and nodded her head.

Now it was his turn to look relieved. "Then it wasn't something I said!"

That surprised her. How could Stephen think that she had been so quiet and reserved because of something that he had said or done? He had been nothing short of the perfect escort, kind and attentive during the buggy rides home. "Oh no!" she gushed but quickly stopped herself from saying anything else, lest he'd think she was too forward.

"Gut!" he said back cheerfully. "Then I may take you home tonight, ja?"

She felt as if the weight of the world was lifted from her shoulders. Perhaps things would work out all right, she thought. After all, Susie hadn't ruined his interest in her. "Oh ja!" she replied. There was nothing more that she would like than to ride home with Stephen Esh. "That would be right nice," she added softly.

Once again, he brushed his hand against her arm. "Remember something, Priscilla Smucker."

"What's that?" she asked, lifting her eyes to stare up at him.

"When someone makes accusations, it is often a mirror into their own soul," he said. "And just as often, that they are speaking of their own sins." With that, he winked at her. "I'll see you after the singing."

Elated, Priscilla watched as he rejoined his friends, pausing just once to look back at her over his shoulder. His smile gave her strength and she lifted her chin to join the group of girls that were standing nearby. She ignored those that chose to walk away, making their support of Susie Byler far too apparent. Priscilla knew that the community was well aware of the false bravado behind Susie's accusations and she felt better at once.

It warmed her heart to know that there were so many good practicing Christians in their community, despite the sad feeling that tried to fight its way into her heart. She felt sorry for the handful of people that fell by the wayside, choosing to believe the false accusations from Susie Byler who was clearly driven by envy at the attention that was given to Priscilla, Anna, and anyone else who would dare to enter their own goods into the charity dinner. Would they ever know the truth?

Chapter Eight

It was the day of the charity dinner. Priscilla had spent the last week caring for her garden and praying that nothing more would happen with Susie Byler. It had come back to Priscilla that Susie Byler was still hopping mad, demanding that Polly not accept Priscilla's entry into the charity event, even going to far as to start her own charity event if Polly would not listen to her.

Priscilla had only shook her head when Anna and Sarah came by the Smucker farm earlier that week and told her about what was happening beyond her daed's lane. "I don't think I want to hear anymore," Priscilla said quietly. Her heart broke for Susie Byler, knowing that she was suffering and needed the hand of God to help her through whatever was the root of her problem. "I feel much better now that I am avoiding her."

Sarah had frowned. "I wish Polly could avoid her. That Susie is constantly at her daed's farm and making such silly demands."

"She does realize that this is for a good cause, ja?" Anna had asked.

Sarah rolled her eyes. "She's claiming that Polly is persecuting her."

Even Priscilla had gasped when she heard that. "Is she comparing herself to...?" She couldn't even finish the sentence.

To claim to be persecuted was a mighty large statement. After all, the Amish were of the Anabaptist movement that had been persecuted for hundreds of years before they moved to America in the 1700s. Priscilla often read from the worn and tattered book, The Martyr's Mirror, a book that every Amish household kept on their bookshelf. She had always been fascinated with the strength of the few who were tortured, beaten, and burned for their beliefs in the Anabaptist movement. But to think that Susie Byler was comparing herself to those martyrs? Over tomatoes?

Now, as Priscilla stood at the edge of the tomato patch, looking at her creations, she bowed her head in prayer to thank God for all that He had done and to also ask that He help Susie Byler work her way through her own ordeal. She knew that Susie needed their prayers, not their scorn. Perhaps God would show some extra mercy on Susie to help her through whatever was really bothering her.

"Everything looks amazing, Priscilla," her mamm said as she walked around the barn toward the garden. In the early morning sun, her mamm looked lovely. Her green dress and black apron contrasted with Priscilla's, which was burgundy today. Her mamm stood at the edge of the tomato patch and surveyed it, a smile on her face. "You sure have worked hard on this."

"No harder than others, I suppose," Priscilla said modestly. "And it's for such a good cause."

Her mamm took a deep breath. "Well, I sure do know that it can be hard to stick to your morals when you are being unfairly attacked."

Priscilla gasped. "You knew?"

With a smile, her mamm glanced up at the rising sun. "You know how that Amish grapevine works, Priscilla. I figured you'd talk to me if you needed advice." She glanced back at Priscilla. "But I see that you already knew how to handle it without my guidance."

Priscilla blushed. It meant a lot to Priscilla to know that her mamm had believed in her and approved of how the situation had been handled. Priscilla had never once thought that her handling of the situation was a reflection on her family and her faith. She now understood the magnitude of the test that had been placed before her.

"Oh mamm," Priscilla said, trying to hid the overwhelming emotion that was creeping into her chest. "I've had sixteen years of love and guidance from you. It made it so much easier to know how to handle the situation, I reckon."

It was Mamm's turn to flush.

Leaning against the hoe, Priscilla turned her attention back to the garden. "All that work and it comes down to today," she said. She felt butterflies in her stomach, wondering if anyone would even buy her tomatoes. If no one bought them, that would certainly satisfy Susie Byler. "If even one person is helped just a little from this charity event, it will all have been worth it."

"Your reasons behind doing this are pure, Priscilla," her mamm said. "Somewhere in the world there is a person who will be a little more fortunate today than yesterday because of your heart."

Her mamm's words struck a chord. Priscilla had never thought about it that way. Suddenly, she realized that all of the emotional turmoil that she had been feeling for the past few weeks was worth it. Originally, she hadn't started her garden for any other reason than her own love of gardening and growing food that her family would enjoy. But, now that she was able to use that passion to touch others, she wanted to do just that.

Unlike Susie Byler who was focused on raising the most money, Priscilla only cared about how she could help others. Stephen Esh's words about accusations mirroring the soul of the accuser returned to her and she realized how very powerful that statement had been.

"I suppose it's time to pull the tomatoes from the vines and pack them in the basket. Would you like to help me?" she asked her mamm.

"Ja," her mamm responded. "I'd like nothing more than to help you, daughter."

They spent the next hour in the garden, working silently side-by-side. The juicy, red tomatoes were plucked from the vine and set gently into a box. Priscilla also pulled some beets and carrots, deciding to include those in the donation as well. She loved the way that the dirt clung to the vegetables when she pulled them from the ground. Brushing the dirt off, she admired the beauty of the long orange carrots and dusty red beets. She hoped that they tasted as good as they looked for whoever would bid on her donation today.

After washing and drying each of the tomatoes, carrots, and beets, Priscilla set them carefully on the table while she prepared the bushel basket. She had an idea to decorate the basket and had spent a few evenings knitting a small red, white, and pink square. Now, she placed the square inside the bushel basket, letting the corners drop over the sides. Then, she laid the tomatoes inside, one on top of another, ever so gently so that they wouldn't bruise.

She affixed the bunch of carrots to the side of the basket so that the tomatoes that were filled at the top looked as though they were resting on them. The green carrot tops were gently woven around the rim of the basket, the perfect contrast to the red tomatoes and brown basket. The beets were placed at the back of the basket in a similar fashion. She took a step back and frowned, surveying her creation. Pretty is as pretty does, she reminded herself with a sigh. It would just have to do.

"Looks just right."

Priscilla turned around and smiled at her brother. "It'll have to do, ja?"

Jonas nodded his head. "Your hard work and true nature shows through, Priscilla. That's all that matters, not?" He didn't wait for her to respond. "Now, I do believe I'd like the honor of taking you and your donation from the tomato patch over to the church so that they have it ready for the dinner. Would you allow me that privilege?"

She laughed at his theatrics. He was such a good brother and would make a wonderful husband to some lucky Amish woman one day. "I would be happy to ride along with you," she said.

"That's gut," he said, reaching for his hat as he walked toward the door. "Especially since I'm sure it will be Stephen Esh who brings you home!"

Priscilla's mouth fell open and she was about to say something in reply but Jonas dashed out the door.

Chapter Nine

The church was filled with people that Priscilla had never seen before. It was a small brick church with four steps that led to the front door. Outside, there were ten tents that were raised in the parking lot and onto the grounds behind the church. Under each tent were rows of tables. Priscilla knew that her bushel of tomatoes was inside and waiting for bidding. It made her nervous to know that so many people were watching the bidding tonight, mostly because of Susie Byler. But she was also very proud that Polly Yoder had stood her ground and been so diplomatic, focusing on the end goal...helping others...rather than catering to the whims of one person.

She stood on the side of the church grounds, amazed at the number of people who had showed up for the charity event. Tickets for the noon-day meal were being sold by the dozens and families were perusing the aisles of donated food to bid on the items. Priscilla couldn't believe how much had been donated. But she was pleased to know that all of the money would go toward helping others. The Mennonites were so good about reaching beyond their community to help those in need. She knew that the Amish helped people, too, but it was mostly the local people. If someone's barn burned down, the Amish were right there to help rebuild the building. If a father died, the people in the church district were the first to stand in line to help with chores and finances, should the need call for such extreme measures.

The tents that had the charity items were filled with people. There were Amish women in different color dresses and bare feet walking along the tables, looking at the items on display. There were canned goods, homemade cheese, baskets full of fruits and vegetables. In another tent, there were breads, pastries and whoopie pies. In yet one more tent, there were quilts, afghans and potholders, all created and donated by the people in the local community.

For the Amish and Mennonites that didn't farm, this was a wonderful way to purchase items for their families while helping those in need. With such large families and with the shrinking amount of farmland, many Amish were turning toward carpentry or shop jobs, jobs that kept them from growing their own food to preserve for winter consumption. Priscilla was touched when she realized that some of those in need were in their own community.

Out of curiosity, Priscilla walked through the tent with the vegetables. She was pleased to see that there were lots of bushels of tomatoes and other vegetables, several that were decorated as pretty as her basket. She breathed a sigh of relief to know that she was not alone. Hopefully that would calm Susie Byler and her jealous bullying. Certainly she couldn't be upset now, especially since there were so many donations.

In front of each donation was a sign-up sheet. People would move through the tent and write their donation on the sheet of paper. After the meal was served, the sheets would be pulled up and the winners would be announced. Priscilla was even more pleased to see that all of the sheets had donations written down on them. The Mennonites were raising quite a bit of money to help others, she thought.

"Priscilla!" someone called out.

She turned around and saw Anna hurrying toward her.

"Did you see who bid on your tomatoes?"

"Why no, I didn't," she said. She hadn't thought to look at who had bid on her donation. That didn't seem important. But apparently something had happened that made Anna bring it up.

Anna grabbed her arm and dragged Priscilla back toward the vegetable tent. As they walked, she whispered in her ear, "If Susie Byler was upset before, this should really send her over the edge." But there was no joy in Anna's voice.

Inside the tent, Priscilla saw that several people were standing around the table in front of her donation. The women looked up and smiled at Priscilla, backing away so that she could see the donation sheet.

"Seems your tomatoes are quite popular this year," one of the women said.

"I can't imagine why," Priscilla said modestly. "They are no better than anyone else's." As she said that, she glanced down at the sheet. There were several names and amounts listed but it was the last name that made her catch her breath: Elias Zook, the bishop. He had bid forty dollars for her basket of tomatoes. Priscilla looked up and stared at Anna. "Forty dollars?"

Anna nodded her head and lowered her voice as they turned to walk back toward the church. "I suppose that's a clear statement that he knows what has been going on and he's publically supporting the truth."

"That's a mighty expensive statement," Priscilla responded, shaking her head.

Inside the church, the people were gathering downstairs for the noon-meal. Priscilla and Anna stood by each other during the silent prayer before the food was ready to be eaten. Then, while the people formed lines and passed along the buffet table, the Amish women started to sing an old German hymn. The men and children joined in, their voices rising in unison while those in line filled their plates and the rest waited for their turn.

After filling her plate, Priscilla sat down at a table where Polly and Sarah were seated. They were laughing and enjoying themselves as they talked with the other girls. People were complimenting Rachel about the beautiful quilt that she had donated. They also praised Linda for her canned goods and Polly for her delicious whoopie pies. Everyone had donated something for the day and was feeling good about the turn-out of guests that had bid on all the items.

It wasn't until after the meal that everyone gathered upstairs. Priscilla stood with her friends, ignoring the stares from the Englischers who had joined the festivities for the day. Despite their curiosity, the Englischers had certainly bid on many of the items that were donated that day, especially the quilts.

"Well, one thing is for sure and certain," Polly said smiling. "We know who bought Priscilla's tomatoes!"

Linda laughed. "Bishop Zook sure seems to like tomatoes to bid so much on yours. Certainly no one else would go up against him."

"And not for more money," Anna nodded. "But that's money raised for the good of the poor."

"Ssssh," Sarah whispered. "They are starting their announcements!"

Everyone quieted down as a man stepped up to a

podium. He cleared his throat and spoke in a loud voice so that everyone could hear. "First, I'd like to thank everyone who donated their goods to help us raise money for the Mennonite Central Committee. All of the donations helped raise money so that we can continue helping those in need around the world. Second, I'd like to thank everyone who turned out today to bid on these items. By bidding on these goods, you have helped us in helping others."

The Mennonite ladies began to carry goods to the podium so that he could read the winners of each item. He started with the pies and breads before moving onto the canned goods and cheese. There were several donations in each category so it took some time to get to the vegetables. Finally, they would end with the highlight of the entire charity dinner: the quilts.

When it was time for the vegetables, Priscilla bit her lip and held Anna's hand. The announcer went through all of the other baskets of vegetables but seemed to be holding back Priscilla's entry. She began to feel nervous and her heart beat inside of her chest. She hadn't seen Susie Byler at the charity dinner but she wasn't really surprised. After all of the fuss that she had made, Susie was certain to not be in the mood for celebration, especially since she had not donated anything this year.

"We saved this last entry because it was quite an interesting situation," the announcer finally said. The Mennonite lady standing next to him held Priscilla's basket. Several people glanced at Priscilla and she shuffled her barefeet in the grass, embarrassed by the attention. The man continued speaking. "There seems to have been a bidding war on this particular donation."

The crowd laughed.

Priscilla looked at Anna, questioning her with a raised eyebrow. "Bidding war?"

Anna laughed and shook her head. "I never heard of such a thing!"

The announcer seemed to delight in the soft murmuring among the crowd and let it continue, building the suspense. "After going back and forth several times with Bishop Zook, I'm pleased to announce that the winner of this basket of tomatoes is Stephen Esh for fifty-two dollars!"

There was a collective gasp among the group. Never in the history of the charity dinner had a basket of tomatoes or any vegetable raised so much money. The big money donations were usually saved for the quilts which would bring in anywhere from two to five hundred dollars. Fifty-two dollars for a basket of tomatoes was unheard of. The crowd applauded and parted as Stephen Esh, a broad grin on his face, walked to the front of the gathering and collected his basket.

"Oh Priscilla!" Anna gasped, clutching her friend's hands. "Can you believe this?"

Priscilla was speechless and felt the color flood to her cheeks. Stephen Esh had bid against the bishop? And so much money? For her tomatoes? "I don't believe it," she murmured, lowering her eyes so that no one would think that she was prideful.

Polly leaned forward. "I'd say that this was the best charity dinner ever, Priscilla. You should feel good about your donation."

But she didn't.

She waited through the announcement of the quilt

winners, applauding along with the rest of the crowd. The quilts were always the highlight of any charity event. Yet, she couldn't wait until it was over. She wanted to leave, to think about what had happened, and to just spend a little time by herself.

Even though there was more fellowship after the reading of the winners, Priscilla snuck away, walking down the lane toward her daed's farm. It was a good three miles away but she didn't mind. She was looking forward to the cool summer breeze on her face and quiet of simply being alone.

So much had happened and much of it seemed like a dream. She couldn't believe how poorly Susie Byler had behaved. Enough people in the community knew about it and that was certain to raise eyebrows. Even though Susie deserved whatever discussion was certain to follow from the bishop, Priscilla couldn't bring herself to feel anything less than sorry for the troubled girl. She just hoped that the rest of the community was as forgiving as she was feeling.

A buggy pulled along side her and she stepped to the side of the road, allowing it to pass. But it didn't.

"Priscilla Smucker!"

She looked up, surprised that someone was calling her name. It was Stephen Esh, riding in an open top buggy, her basket of tomatoes on the seat beside him. She blushed and looked down at her bare feet.

"I've been looking for you," he said, his eyes twinkling and a broad smile on his face. "Your daed said you had left after the quilt announcements. I just had to come after you."

"Why?" she asked.

"Well," he said, gesturing to the basket of tomatoes. "I

wanted to see if you might have some ideas of what to do with all of these lovely red tomatoes that I bought!" She smiled at his joke, the color flooding to her cheeks, once again. He seemed to have that habit of making her blush. And it sure looked like he enjoyed it. He stopped the buggy and, after pulling in the brake, moved the basket to the floor of the buggy. He patted the seat next to him. "Hop in and I'll give you a ride home."

Once she was settled in the buggy beside him, she lifted her eyes and met his gaze. "You spent an awful lot of money on that basket," she said. "Why would you do that?"

Stephen made a face at her, pretending to frown but his lips were smiling. "Why wouldn't I? I couldn't have the bishop enjoying my girl's tomatoes!"

She caught her breath. *My girl?* Had he really said that? She felt her heart flutter and her blood began to course through her veins. Was she truly going to be Stephen's Priscilla? By calling her that, she knew what he was thinking. "I see," she said softly. When he didn't say anything, she looked back up to see him watching her.

He was gauging her reaction. It must have taken quite a bit of courage for him to say that to her, especially since they had only been riding together a few times. Now, he was waiting. Recognizing his anticipation, she took a deep breath and, with a smile on her face, she nodded and said, "I suppose that wouldn't be proper after all, now would it?"

Stephen laughed, a look of relief washing over his face. He unlocked the brake so that the horse could move forward. "No it wouldn't," he said and smiled to himself as the buggy moved down the road toward the Smucker's farm.

Chapter Ten

The following week, Priscilla could hardly wait until church Sunday. She had helped her daed and brothers with cutting and baling hay during the week. It was an exhausting few days but she loved every minute of it. Being near her brothers and daed, enjoying the meals that her mamm made, and helping work the fields that God blessed them with...it all made everything right. Plus, the words "my girl" rang in her ears. When she was tired and sore, she thought of those words and felt inspired to try harder.

When Sunday came, she made certain to get up extra early to help her daed with the morning chores. Then, after working with her mamm in the kitchen to prepare breakfast, she hurried upstairs to get ready for church. It was a hot day and the second floor of the house was especially hot. She knew that it would be a long, hot morning at the service. When she walked back downstairs, she was glad that it was cooler there.

"Going to be a hot one, ja?" her daed said, splashing water on his face at the kitchen sink.

"I sure hope they have the service in the barn," Mamm said. "Cooler when the doors are open, no doubt." She looked up as Priscilla walked into the kitchen. "Mayhaps after service you might take Elsie's *kinner* to the pond for a dip to cool off."

Priscilla nodded. She was glad that her mamm had suggested that. She would love to cool off in the pond down the road and the *kinner* would enjoy it, too. "That might be the perfect thing to do on a day like today."

"Bet you won't be alone at that pond," her daed quipped,

his eyes bright and twinkling. "Probably have to battle to find a free spot to dip your big toe!"

As luck would have it, the service was, indeed, being held in the barn. The doors were open and there was a nice cross breeze that helped to keep it cool. Priscilla sat next to Anna and Sarah, singing the first hymn from the Ausbund as the ministers left the barn to privately discuss who would give that day's sermons. She was always amazed that the decision for the sermon was done right then and there, as the congregation sang the opening hymn. Yet, without doubt, whoever was selected always had a relevant topic and lively sermon, complete with quotations from the scripture. Being chosen to lead the church must be a heavy burden as well as a blessing, she often thought.

She felt someone staring at her and, when she looked up, she noticed that Stephen Esh, who was sitting along the back wall, had his eyes upon her. When he noticed that she was returning his gaze, he smiled softly and gave a single nod in recognition. *My girl*, she thought and the color rose to her cheeks as she quickly looked away.

When the ministers returned to the gathering, Priscilla wondered who had been chosen to present the sermon. She liked to watch their faces, to see if she could determine whom it was. Most of the time, she was incorrect. But it was a fun game that she liked to play, hoping to one day fine-tune her skills at reading their expressions.

She was surprised when Bishop Zook stood up. He cleared his throat and seemed to be deep in thought as he paced the floor and stared among the congregation. Priscilla wondered what he was thinking. Even Anna seemed nervous as she watched her uncle. He was silent longer than usual and the congregation began to sit up straighter, watching him and waiting.

"Competition!"

Everyone stood up straight and stared at him, surprised at the word that he shouted. His eyes were blazing and his expression was stern. Priscilla felt her heart drop. She suspected she knew where this sermon was headed and she lowered her eyes. Could he truly be so upset over losing the basket of tomatoes to Stephen Esh that he'd give an entire sermon about it?

"Competition is good for the world," he said, his voice still stern. "It helps them progress with their worldly lives. Competition has helped the Englischer create new inventions...cars, televisions, telephones, computers. Competition has helped their businesses grow and their families acquire a comfortable lifestyle." He paused, his eyes rolling across the eyes that were staring at him. "But competition is not good for our community!"

There was a soft murmuring among the people and Priscilla noticed that several were squirming on the hard, wooden benches. She wanted to look over at Stephen but was too afraid to do so.

"Competition is prideful," the bishop continued. "I have personally witnessed this pride. I am here to stand before you to make it stop. We will not tolerate pride among our members. Pride sets one member above another. Pride tears down others in our community. Pride is the one thing that destroys our chosen way of life!"

He reached for a glass of water that someone had placed on a hay bale near where he was standing. He took his time drinking from it, his eyes still fierce and animated. No one moved. They watched him, waiting for his next remarks. Priscilla glanced over at Stephen Esh and was surprised to see that there was a hint of a smile on his face. She wondered if he was daydreaming for he certainly couldn't be hearing what the bishop was saying.

"We work together as a people. We help others, not turn our backs. We support each other, not tear each other down," he said. Priscilla frowned. Was he still talking about Stephen? The bishop took a deep breath before he continued.

"'They also boast themselves as Christians,
And yet do not speak truthfully,
One recognizes it by their craftiness,
Which revels where they are.
The tree is known by the fruits,
The wicked will be rooted out
And burned with eternal fire.

Therefore, King Solomon says,
A beautiful woman without discretion
Is like a swine adorned with gold!
Truly it brings her no benefit,
Even though she carries it upon her nose.
She fouls it constantly with dung,
Therewith she makes mischief.'"[2]

Everyone stared at the bishop, their eyes wide and faces pale. Even Priscilla was stunned. Clearly he was no longer talking about Stephen Esh, if he had been at all. Suddenly, she had a feeling that this sermon was going in a completely different direction.

---

[2] Songs of the Ausbund, Song 69 Verse 21-22

"There will be no more competition," he said strongly. "We work together to help each other. If pride gets in the way, it is our responsibility to help that person see the errors of his or her ways. To not do so is to be just as guilty of pride."

Again, he cleared his throat and reached for the water. No one moved as they waited.

"Charity begins at home," he said. "With ourselves. There is no room for accusations, lies, and bullying among our church members." He narrowed his eyes. "That's right. Bullying. This sin of pride led to bullying among some of our youths. I will hear of this no more! In all my years, I have never heard of bullying among our members. That was strictly something that happened in the world of the Englische. But these past few weeks, our youth have been bullied because of a charity drive at the Mennonite church! The root of the bullying was jealousy over competition!" He raised his hand and lifted his eyes. "Where was the love of the Lord during this time?"

Priscilla paled. She wished that she could turn around to look at Susie Byler. But she knew better than to do that.

Suddenly, the bishop softened his tone. "But we forgive. That is what we do. We forgive." The words hung in the air and he let them linger there before he began to quote from the Ausbund once more.

>"'If you see him transgress,
>Committing a sin against you,
>Kindly you shall beseech him,
>Point out to him in love
>Between him and you alone
>Does he then repent,

You shall be satisfied.'" [3]

He let those words sink in giving the congregation time to reflect on them before he continued. "We forgive and let the sinners repent. If that person does not hear you, you must reveal the matter to the church so that we can approach that person to point out the need to ask for God's grace."

The bishop narrowed his eyes. "But if the sinner does not repent and does not listen to the church," he said, his voice stern once more.

"'From him do separate yourself
Indeed the very same hour,
Keep him as a heathen
As Christ has proclaimed.
Paul also said without deceit and craftiness
Put him away from among you
Whoever is disobedient.'"[4]

The bishop paused. The message was clear. Even though Susie Byler had not become a baptized member of the church yet, the bishop was instructing everyone to help guide her. If she didn't repent, she would not be permitted to join the church and that would be almost as bad as being shunned. "We do not do this in anger or to punish. We do this without gossip or reproach," he said as he lowered his voice. "Indeed, we do this in love."

When the service was finally over, Priscilla could hardly contain herself. She wanted to speak to Anna and Sarah privately but knew better than to do so during the fellowship

---

[3] Songs of the Ausbund, Song 56 Verse 4

[4] Songs of the Ausbund, Song 56 Verse 8

time. She didn't want to appear as a gossiper but she was anxious and on edge. She simply couldn't believe that the bishop had been so bold and so brazen as to address the issue in such a public manner.

It was clear that she wasn't the only one. No one else spoke about the sermon. In fact, it was obvious that everyone was avoiding any discussion about what the bishop had said. Instead, everyone was reflecting on his words and doing their best to appear extra friendly and kind toward everyone. Even Susie Byler appeared withdrawn and subdued. Perhaps the bishop got through to her, Priscilla thought as she refilled the water glasses for the men during the first seating of the fellowship meal.

"Danke," Stephen said as Priscilla refilled his water glass. "I will see you later, ja?"

She smiled, lowering her eyes that he had asked her that in front of his peers. She noticed that her brother raised an eyebrow. "I'll be at the singing, if that's what you mean," she responded coyly. She didn't want people gossiping about her budding relationship with Stephen Esh, although he didn't seemed to mind if people knew that she was his girl.

"Heard you might take your sister's *kinner* to the pond," he said.

Priscilla glanced at her brother and he shrugged his shoulders sheepishly. "Ja," she admitted. "Would be helpful to watch them for Elsie a little."

Stephen nodded. "I was thinking about heading over there myself." He ignored the snickers from the other young men seated around him. "Mayhaps you could use some help with the *kinner*?"

This time, she smiled at him without feeling self-conscious. "That would be right gut, Stephen Esh." She continued moving down the table to continue refilling the men's water glasses. Now she was really looking forward to the afternoon with Elsie's *kinner* since Stephen was going to come along to help her.

Chapter Eleven

The big oak tree by the pond cast a wide circle of shade on the grass. True to Daed's prediction, there were many other people already wading into the water while the children played and splashed each other. Priscilla set down the picnic basket that her mamm had packed with sandwiches, fresh peaches, and two jars of lemonade. She had even put in a shoofly pie for the children to enjoy after they had eaten their food.

Priscilla found a spot in the shade and spread out the old quilt that she had carried along. It was nicer to sit on the quilt than on the scratchy grass. Katie, Ruth Ann, and Ben were holding hands and splashing in the water. Priscilla watched them, her arms wrapped around her knees. She loved seeing how nicely they played. Their laughter warmed her heart. After such a crazy few weeks, she was glad to start feeling relaxed again.

"Did you just get here?"

Priscilla looked up to see Stephen Esh standing under the tree. "We did, ja."

His knees cracked as he bent down beside her. "Brought some ice cream." He set a brown bag down on the ground. "Thought the little ones might like it but they should eat it soon. Will melt quickly."

"That was right thoughtful," she said. His kind gesture touched her. Waving to the *kinner*, she called them back to the blanket. Katie plopped down next to her and grinned a toothless smile at Stephen Esh. "You have a special treat today," Priscilla said. "Stephen brought you some ice cream."

Ben whooped and did a little dance, causing a round of giggles from Katie and Ruth Ann. Even Stephen smiled at the little boy's enthusiasm.

"Normally we'd wait until after our food but, seeing that it's so hot, I don't think we have much choice," Priscilla said.

While the children ate their ice cream, Stephen sat down on the quilt next to Priscilla. He sat close enough that his arm brushed against hers. She liked how attentive he was toward her. She knew that many Amish youth were not as comfortable around women and were shy. She was sure glad that Stephen Esh didn't behave in such an awkward manner.

"What did you think of the bishop's sermon today?" he asked as he bit into his own ice cream bar.

"Oh," she said, surprised by the question. She hadn't expected him to come right out and ask her about it. "I...well..." she stammered.

He laughed at her. "That's what I thought you'd say." He turned to look at her. "You handled yourself quite well during that.." He hesitated. What should one call what happened? "Bizarre event," he finally settled on. "It's admirable that you maintained your distance and refused to take her bait."

"Stephen," she said softly. "I don't know if I'm comfortable talking about this."

He nodded. "Understood and that's exactly what I mean. I just want you to know that you proved yourself to be a good Christian during it and I, for one, was proud of you."

"Proud?" she whispered. "I think we have learned about pride."

He shook his head. "Oh no, there's a big difference, Priscilla." He finished his ice cream and wiped his hands on his pants. "Pride in oneself is sinful. But being proud of others is natural. Don't confuse the two."

She digested that for a minute. How many times had her mamm looked at her with pride in her eyes? Could that feeling be the type of good pride that Stephen meant? There were even times when Priscilla watched Katie, Ruth Ann, and Ben interact and she was proud of their good, Christian values. They rarely fought and were usually most helpful...well, not always feisty Katie but she was still a good girl. Perhaps Stephen was right.

"I guess you have a good point," she said. But she was still embarrassed that he had confided in her. No one had ever come right out to say that they were proud of her. Not in so many words.

"The trick now..." he said, waving his finger in the air. "Is how we can all prove to Susie that we support her in order to help her." He rested his chin on his knees. "I heard that the bishop went to her home and talked to her. Hopefully she will learn her lesson and be a nicer person."

But Priscilla wasn't so certain. To be honest, Susie hadn't looked remorseful at all after the sermon. She had helped with the fellowship meal in silence, her eyes narrow and her chin lifted high. "We can only hope so," she said slowly. "And pray."

For the rest of the afternoon, Priscilla and Stephen played with the kinner in the pond. There was a lot of laughter and splashing, chasing and dunking. By the time the afternoon began to wan, Priscilla was pleased to see that all three children looked tired and worn out. They would sleep well tonight, despite the unusual heat wave that was pressing down upon them.

Stephen walked with them back toward their farms. He carried the quilt while Priscilla carried the now empty basket. They walked the *kinner* across the road to Elsie's house, laughing as the children gushed about their exciting afternoon at the pond. Then, as they crossed the street back to her daed's, Stephen seemed to slow his pace. "It was a great afternoon, Priscilla Smucker," he said.

"That it was," she admitted. "I can't thank you enough for bringing ice cream. That was such a special treat, Stephen."

He smiled back at her but didn't comment about that. Instead, he asked, "I trust you'll be at the singing tonight?"

She nodded. "Ja, I'll be riding over with Jonas."

He frowned for a moment, looking up into the sky. He appeared to be thinking of something as he accessed the still hot sun that was slowly making its way to the horizon. "It sure is awful hot to ride over to the singing in a closed buggy, don't you think?"

She watched him carefully, wondering what he was planning. She was starting to know him well enough to figure out that he spoke with purpose. "It might cool down," she said slowly, still watching him.

He shook his head. "Might be better if you rode over to the singing in an open buggy," he said then turned to look at her. She recognized the mischievous sparkle in his blue eyes. "I could pick you up in mine, if you'd like."

She tried not to smile and lowered her eyes. "I suppose that might be nice, too."

A broad grin broke onto his face. He handed her the quilt when she was ready to go into the house. "That might just be the ending to the most perfect day," he said. Then, hesitating, he added as if an after-thought, "So far anyway. I have a suspicion that they will only get better from here."

She laughed as he hurried down the lane, pausing once to turn back and wave. He had left his horse and buggy in the shade of the tree by the pond and needed to return there to fetch it.

Walking back down the lane, Priscilla paused as she passed her garden. It was still growing well, despite the heat. She noticed that there were new green tomatoes growing on the stalks. God is amazing, she thought. With a little love and a lot of hard work, the plants would continue to provide new tomatoes for the rest of the summer. She would continue to work in the garden, nurturing all of the vegetables. She'd can as much as she would be able to for the winter, so that her entire family would enjoy them.

Sighing, she shut her eyes and lifted her face to the sun. It was amazing to her how much had happened in the past few weeks and all of it centered around the tomato patch. Indeed, for when she thought that she had only been planting vegetables, she had truly been planting the seeds for her new life.

Smiling, she hurried down the rest of the lane, eager to tell her mamm about the afternoon while they prepared the family supper meal. Then, she had to get ready for the singing since Stephen Esh would be certain to pick her up earlier so that they could spend more time alone. He was right, she thought as she climbed the steps to the front porch, this was indeed the perfect day.

Book Discussion Questions

By Pamela Jarrell, Administrator of The Whoopie Pie Book Club on Facebook

Question #1: What did you feel was the greatest strength of this book?

Question #2: We know that Susie was jealous and wanted everyone's attention, but why do you think that her biggest target was Priscilla?

Question #3: What do you think that Susie's underlying issues were to cause her to act the way she does?

Question #4: Do you think that Polly & Anna handled their part of the situations correctly?

Question #5: Do you think that in the background, Stephen Esh may have had his eye on Priscilla for a long time and was waiting for her to turn 16?

Question #6: Do you feel that the author's knowledge of the Amish and this morale situation was well portrayed in this book?

Question #7: Where do you vision that this story goes after the novella ends?

Love reading Amish romances and Amish Christian fiction? Please join the Whoopie Pie Book Club Group on Facebook where members share stories, photos, book reviews, and have weekly book club discussions.

ABOUT THE AUTHOR

The Preiss family emigrated from Europe in 1705, settling in Pennsylvania as the area's first wave of Mennonite families. Sarah Price has always respected and honored her ancestors through exploration and research about her family's history and their religion. At nineteen, she befriended an Amish family and lived on their farm throughout the years. Twenty-five years later, Sarah Price splits her time between her home outside of New York City and an Amish farm in Lancaster County, PA where she retreats to reflect, write, and reconnect with her Amish friends and Mennonite family.

Find Sarah Price on Facebook and Goodreads!
Learn about upcoming books, sequels, series, and contests!

Contact the author at sarahprice.author@gmail.com.
Visit her weblog at http://sarahpriceauthor.wordpress.com or on Facebook at www.facebook.com/fansofsarahprice.

Made in the USA
Charleston, SC
27 November 2012